SOME SWELL PUP

SOME SWELL PUP

or Are You Sure You Want a Dog?

Story by Maurice Sendak and Matthew Margolis

Pictures by Maurice Sendak

FARRAR, STRAUS AND GIROUX · NEW YORK

HEH HEH

Library of Congress catalog card number: 75-42870
Published simultaneously in Canada
by McGraw-Hill Ryerson Ltd., Toronto
Printed in the United States of America
by Pearl Pressman Liberty
Bound by A. Horowitz and Son
Typography by Atha Tehon
Calligraphy by Jeanyee Wong
First edition, 1976

For Connie, Erda, Io, and Aggie M.S.

For my son, Jesse M.M.

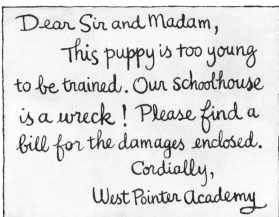

AND SO, NEXT DAY . . .

THAT NIGHT...

SO THEY WENT TO SLEEP AND DREAMED...

THE BOY'S DREAM

AND IN THE MORNING . . .

SO...